Manners

First published in 2004 by
Franklin Watts
96 Leonard Street
London
EC2A 4XD

Franklin Watts Australia
45–51 Huntley Street
Alexandria
NSW 2015

Text © Hilary Robinson 2004
Illustration © Jane Abbott 2004

A CIP catalogue record for this book is available
from the British Library.

ISBN 0 7496 5869 X (hbk)
ISBN 0 7496 5873 8 (pbk)

Series Editor: Jackie Hamley
Series Advisor: Dr Barrie Wade
Cover Design: Jason Anscomb
Design: Peter Scoulding

Printed in Hong Kong / China

With love to Damien, Molly and Zachary – J.A.

For Isobel and Guy – H.R.

HOPSCOTCH

How to Teach a Dragon Manners

by Hilary Robinson and Jane Abbott

W

FRANKLIN WATTS

LONDON • SYDNEY

When Mabel's dragon came for tea
Each afternoon at half past three,

He'd sniff and turn his long nose up

At apple juice poured in his cup.

He'd sulk and look down at his feet,
When given beans with cold
roast meat.

He got so cross, one salad day:

"Rabbit food! Take it away!"

Mabel was so happy when

Her dragon said that he'd like ten

Bowls of jelly and bones to gnaw –

But then:

"I'm not that hungry anymore."

Mabel's face got hot and red.
She was so cross she loudly said:
"Dragon, here's a pen to make a list
Of all the meals you can't resist.

"There's the bus to take you down
To do the shopping in the town.

"Here's your coat and take this sack
To bring the heavy shopping back.

"Here's the book on how to make
Your own hot meals and

chocolate cake.
And when you've done, please

don't forget...

"To wash up all the plates and pans,

And throw away the tins and cans.

"Then sweep
the floor...

...and wipe the table!

Is that okay with you?" said Mabel.

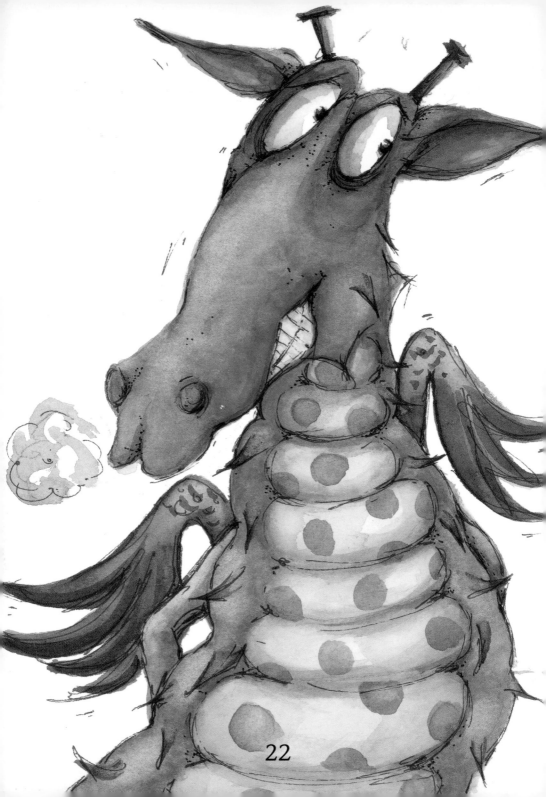

Mabel's dragon thought for a while
And then he whispered with a smile:

"Please may I have fruit and fish
Piled up high upon my dish?

"And for a tasty teatime treat,

May I have ice cream for my sweet?"

Mabel was surprised to see
Her dragon eat up all his tea.

He mopped his lips and said:

"Dear Mabel,

If I may now leave the table,

I'd like to take my plates and cup

And show my thanks by...

...washing up!"

Hopscotch has been specially designed to fit the requirements of the National Literacy Strategy. It offers real books by top authors and illustrators for children developing their reading skills.

There are 25 Hopscotch stories to choose from: